The Adventures of Flowerfox

Praise for The Adventures of Flowerfox

"Wise, heartwarming and beautifully illustrated tale which invites the reader onto a
journey of discovering the wonders of life and finding one's place in the world.
The main character's honesty and ingenious curiosity allow him to undergo a series of life's
transformations and find his own identity under the guidance and wisdom of the natural
world passed onto him by the universe's sages: Moon and Sun.
His innocent yet inquisitive mind allows Flowerfox to discover a world full of beauty and
wonder and to learn about the everchanging essence of nature. His compassionate
predisposition and ability to listen let him tune into others and soak in a plentitude of
perspectives while teaching him a relevance of respect.
Finally, his open and warm heart open him up to the experiences of love and friendships
which allow him to grow and mature but, as with everything in life, attachment to others
comes with fear and loss not spared to Flowerfox. The joys and sorrows of life turn into
a lesson about the importance of personal growth and nourishing meaningful
connections with others while being immersed in the wisdom of nature and universe
which provide a safe space for everyone who is open to accept it.
A beautiful story of search for meaning and importance of belonging."
--Marta Kunecka, Ph.D Philosophy, Oregon State University

"A universal tale filled with endearing characters. Flowerfox speaks to the condition of the human heart."
--Allyson Ramage

"A touching and honest look at life, love, and grieving. Approachable for all ages."
--Greg Ramage

The Adventures of Flowerfox

Nymphette

A STORY FOR ALL AGES

Maria Orr

SILVERMOON
Arts & Publishing

Silvermoon Arts and Publishing

The Adventures of Flowerfox

A Story for All Ages

Written and Illustrated
by
Maria Orr

Silvermoon Arts and Publishing

Editor, Book Formatting, Cover: Cleone Lyvonne Reed, MSE
Hardcover ISBN 13: 979-821813-021-3
Paperback ISBN: 979-821813-018-3
Library of Congress Control Number: 2023900650
Manufactured, Typeset, and Printed in the United States of America

Dedication

This book is dedicated to all
who are grieving losses
they thought they could not endure,
and trying to find a path
back to beauty and joy.
You are not alone.

Acknowledgments

I am eternally grateful to the Hospice of Santa Cruz County organization, where I was blessed to train as a grief counselor, as well as my clients in the years since, who have taught me so much.

I must also thank my friends Marta and Sophie Kunecka as well as Allyson and Greg Ramage, who graciously read the manuscript and encouraged me to get it published. Their support gave me encouragement to share it with a wider audience. I am equally grateful to Clara Abigail, who did an astute and encouraging initial edit. Cleone Reed believed in the book and kindly took it on to design, final edit, and format. Thank you, Cleone!

My daughters, Adrienne Battle and Stephanie Battle Broce, gave me support and encouragement, and Stephanie's reading of the book was key. Thank you, girls. You will never know what you mean to me.

My late mother Kathleen Orr, my most demanding critic, gave me her feedback and helped me clarify my vision of the book. She also enjoyed the illustrations I was able to share with her before she died, and I still miss sending her pictures of my art. Her contributions helped shape me as an artist, writer, therapist, and human being. I give her gratitude and honor.

I also am grateful to the members of the Free Reference Photos for Artists Facebook group, particularly DeAnn Hope, Deborah Coker, Raija Malin, and the other photographers who graciously provided reference photos for some of the illustrations.

I wish to thank my siblings, Suzanne McGuire, Tony Orr, Bethe Sailer, and Erin Orr, with whom I have shared some of my most devastating losses, and who remind me that despite the passing of both of our parents, we are not orphans. I also wish to thank my cousin Amy, whose grace in surviving the worst catastrophes inspires me.

Words cannot describe my gratitude to my husband Greg McKenzie, who has given me unfailing love and support throughout this process.

Finally, I give my deepest thanks to the soul companions, human and otherwise, who, by leaving when it was time, taught me that I could survive devastating loss.

Ti amo, and big hugs, to all of you.

Introduction

He was called Flowerfox because, had foxes had a word for it, they would have said he was a poet: he was not only wild but pure at heart in a way that life itself was wild and pure at heart, and the song life made was impossibly sweet to his bones. There was a light in his eyes that was his alone and that he never quite learned to hide, no matter the cost.

He would learn the cost. Foxes mature quickly, and even he would find it hard to be an exception.

Flowerfox was born in a time of change. His mother, Maple, and his father, Rogue, had become companions in a season after fires had swept the forest and fields nearby, but then the winter had come and new growth had already begun. Many animals died or fled, including humans, but they and the other foxes in their small pack (which some humans called a skulk, earth, or leash) had been safe. In time some of those who had left returned, but the hunting was still a bit thin for a while even though each hunter shared the game they had killed. The pack moved north afterwards, and the dens they built were still new when Maple bore a litter of seven pups – four females and three males. Of them all, only four survived that hard time. Flowerfox was too young, then, to understand why.

He remembered meeting the outside world for the first time. It was still cold and there were patches of white crust in shaded places; he learned the white crust was called snow. Gradually it disappeared, and the world grew warmer; he and his littermates grew quickly as food became easier to find and they all learned to hunt. It truly seemed a game at first, in a world filled with play. Rogue and Maple, wise and wary from all they had learned in life, protected their children well, so that most survived their vulnerable infancy.

Rogue was an older and battered fox whose exploits and unlikely survivals were legend in the pack; and Maple, though much younger, had learned a great deal from helping to feed her own littermates. Before too long, the fox children, sleek and strong, were exploring on their own, as fox children do, and Flowerfox loved nothing better than to be out in the world, finding new beauties to savor and marvel at.

Flowerfox and Sun Discuss Their Travels

One day when the air was warmer than it had been for a while, one day when the wind was a breeze and not a gale, one day when the song of birds was loud and the scent of blossoms was delicious, one day when the clouds seemed to melt, Flowerfox had a sudden urge to roll in the grass. He did that, and then he had an urge to practice his pounce jumps.

He did that, and then he ran, everywhere and nowhere, very fast. He did that, and then he sat on his haunches and spread out his beautiful tail and looked up in the sky, tilting his head to let his eyes get used to the brightness of it all.

"Hello, Stranger," he said. "Haven't seen you much lately. Nice to have you back."

"Hello, Flowerfox," Sun said back, in a voice so big some creatures would not have known it was there. "How have you been?"

"I'd like to say same-same, but nothing really is," said Flowerfox, lying down and licking his paws delicately, then looking back at Sun.

"Yes, I think I know what you mean, Flowerfox," said Sun, and a shimmer floated gently through the air.

"You know, it's always different, even when it seems it's not. I like it that you're back, though. How long do you think you'll stay this time?"

"Long enough to see it all through to night, and then long enough day by day to see it all through to the darkest time," said Sun. "What's new?"

"Hmmmmm," said Flowerfox, flexing his claws and checking them for dirt and grass. "Well, some humans left, and others came. There looks to be a fine crop of bunnies this year." Not that he had been alive long enough to know other years, other crops. "You know I'm fond of bunnies. There was a big, big wind that knocked some trees down, and now there are some new open places in the forest. And this apple tree behind me smells delicious – just as delicious as always when it blossoms. What's new with you?"

"Well," said Sun, with just a slight sighing pause, "nothing much, and everything. You know, the longer I travel, the more I see, and the more I notice the little things that change, even from a distance."

"Ah. Do tell," said Flowerfox, and rolled over on his back so Sun could warm his belly.

Sun told him how, day by week and season by year, he saw Earth change slowly – coasts receding, waters rising, big winds becoming storms, and rains leaving some places parched while they gathered to drench others, snows and fires and floods and giant ice melts, plants growing where they hadn't grown since Sun was very young and dying where they had always flourished. And humans, there were always more humans.

"I think some creatures might be frightened by the changes, or sad, or angry, and some don't notice. It's the way things are, after all. But do you know what's really interesting to me?" said Sun to Flowerfox.

"What?" said Flowerfox, very curious now. He rolled back over and sat up, wrapping his feathery tail around him and feeling the breeze ruffle it in a most satisfying way.

"Earth is still so very, very beautiful," said Sun. "Earth is still a place of joy... along with everything else."

Flowerfox had nothing to say to this. He felt Sun's warmth and smelled all the good spring smells and watched the apple blossoms blow away, and he knew Sun was right and nothing more need be said.

"And one more thing," said Sun.

Flowerfox cocked his head, listening.

"Your cousins send their greetings. All of them... and there are a lot of them, as you might recall."

This pleased Flowerfox very much, to think of the little rainforest foxes and the desert foxes and all the other ones around the world saying hello to him specially. He yipped for the pure pleasure of it.

And Sun beamed at him, the way only Sun could do.

Flowerfox and the Frog that Got Away

It was a spring evening, and hearing the frogs sing reminded Flowerfox how empty his stomach really was. He decided it had been too long since he'd had frogs. They were delicious and kind of fun to chase.

As he crept to the water's edge, belly low to the ground, Flowerfox brushed by a tree, and a tiny, startled frog sprang off in front of him. Flowerfox gave chase, but the frog's unpredictable leaps left him behind again and again. While once Flowerfox had been able to hide and lull a frog into leaping into his mouth, he had learned that was extremely rare, because their sight was better than his and their noses just as keen. He gave the chase one more long moment; then he gave up, deciding he'd picked the wrong frog. He hunkered down in the grass to take a brief break.

"Your timing is bad," he heard a tiny voice say. It seemed to be quite close. "And by the way, you should know better. You've missed me before. Also by the way, my name is Verde."

None of this was welcome news to Flowerfox, especially since, although he prided himself on his hunting, he could not bring himself to eat an animal whose name he knew—not even a frog. There

was plenty of game about, and knowing the name of the frog turned the game into it being *Someone*. He exhaled gustily.

"Hello, Verde," he replied. "I'm Flowerfox."

"Listen," Verde told him, "this is the time for our mating. I'll be laying eggs soon. I'm just asking you to wait. I can't keep track of my eggs after I lay them; there are too many. So many neither you nor I could count them, if you know what I mean."

Flowerfox thought about this. If he left Verde alone, it meant in a short time there would be tadpoles... and then froglets. They swam, but he'd had more luck with those. Also, there were plenty of other adult frogs, so he wasn't out of luck; he didn't know any of the others by name.

"All right," Flowerfox said, "but I'm hungry now. It's nice to meet you, Verde. I think I have to get going."

"Okay," Verde responded. "There's just one more thing to remember. Do you like flies?"

"Ewww, no!" This startled Flowerfox. "They're annoying! They're as bad as gnats and other little flying pests!"

"Right," said Verde. "But we love them. They're gourmet treats for us, so remember that the next time you hunt frogs."

This made Flowerfox think again. Frogs were tasty, but he didn't need to eat too many— just a few once in a while. "I'll remember that," he promised.

Later, when he was tired and full after catching a snake and stumbling upon someone else's leftover kill, Flowerfox found a den and curled up to think and nap. The night was full of sounds, but all of them were beautiful to him, and none scared him. He thought about how the tiny tree frog he met could have been his meal, or Flowerfox could have considered making a meal of other creatures... smaller game. I guess we're all hunters, he thought. And sometimes, we're all hunted, too. But not tonight, I hope. He closed his eyes.

No, he told himself, not tonight, and he fell fast asleep.

Bawbbikat and Flowerfox Have a Moment

Of the not-fox cousins Flowerfox knew, Bawbbikat was one he gave most respect and distance to. It wasn't hard, as usually she kept to herself; Bawbbikat had kittens to feed and was an excellent mother as well as a hunter. Flowerfox knew that Bawbbikat could hunt and eat foxes, if she wanted to. If Flowerfox had tracked an animal and then found Bawbbikat got there first, he did not argue. Nor did he, as some unwary foxes might, salivate over the prospect of a kitten meal. He might be ignorant of some things, such as Moon's mysteries, but he was not *that* ignorant. In fact, he went out of his way to give Bawbbikat a wide berth; and he often greeted her as Lady, just to remind her he was neither a threat nor (he hoped) prospective prey.

As spring days lengthened to summer, Flowerfox often found himself in a nearby meadow, chasing rodents, rolling in the grasses and short-lived wildflowers, talking to Sun, and generally enjoying himself. He was doing just this one afternoon when he smelled something. It was Bawbbikat, who somehow was already there. Flowerfox made an attempt to slink away, but she greeted him.

"Good day, Flowerfox," she said, in her voice like water on gravel. "You're looking particularly... well-fed."

Although this was a compliment among cousins, even not-fox cousins, coming from Bawbbikat it seemed to take on an edge in Flowerfox's mind. Turning to face her, he tried to hide his wariness. "Good day, Lady," he replied. "And you, too, and as silent as ever."

"Yes, I see I took you by surprise." Bawbbikat stretched and settled back down into her crouch. She was barely visible now in the tall, yellowing grasses, even to a fox. "You can relax, though. I have already eaten, and my kittens are grown and gone." She yawned. "Besides, there is enough game for us both. You need not fear me *quite* so much, at least while that is true." Bawbbikat gave a laugh, an unsettling sound.

"I'm glad to hear it, Lady," said Flowerfox, and relaxed a bit, but just a bit.

"In fact, if you're hunting," said Bawbbikat, "there is a den of rabbits hereabouts. They would not miss a baby or two, I think."

Flowerfox knew this but didn't quite like to say so. "I thought I might have scented them once or twice," he modestly replied.

Bawbbikat laughed again. "Yes, I'm sure you have. Your nose's fame has spread even to us not-foxes."

Flowerfox could not help the slightest bit of preening at this. "Thank you, Lady. And are all of your kittens well?"

Bawbbikat blinked, very slowly. "Why yes, I believe those that survived are hunting well. I pride myself that most of them survived and now are full grown. I catch sight and scent of them from time to time."

Flowerfox had not thought much about the prospect of having his own pups...something he knew must come to every fox if they lived long enough, which he had every hope of doing. His curiosity arose unbidden. "Lady, I hope you don't think me impertinent, but...what is it like to have your own babies?"

Bawbbikat's eyes narrowed to slits, and then she opened them wide and fixed him in their stare. "It is simply in my nature, something I must do. It takes all my focus and energy while I am doing it. It is immense pleasure—and immense pain. And then they leave my den, and I am back to myself again, until I next accept a mate."

Flowerfox took this in. He wasn't quite sure how to imagine it.

"It will come to you," Bawbbikat said, with just a hint of gentleness, most unusual for her.

"I suppose it will. And what," Flowerfox rushed on, before his fear could stop him, "is it like when one dies?"

"It is the way of things," she said quietly. "It is part of it all. It is the pain, but it passes, for the most part. After all, there are the others to feed and tend."

Surprised by the fact that she had answered the question—as well as by his own daring in asking it—Flowerfox tried to absorb this too.

"That will come to you, too," said Bawbbikat.

They sat in silence for a bit, more companionably than they ever had. Flowerfox closed his eyes, absorbed the warm sunshine, and let what she had told him settle into his brain. A few minutes later, he heard a strange sound.

It was Bawbbikat, purring.

Flowerfox and Moon Talk a Little

It was a bright, warm night, the kind that made Flowerfox's already keen nose tremble. He knew Moon would be there soon, so he found a convenient rock to sit on to watch Moon rise.

It was a beautiful sight, one he never tired of. The sky lightened and the stars faded as the clouds drifted past, thin and silver-white. And then, there Moon was.

Fox pricked his ears as he let moonlight fill his eyes. "Hello, Moon," he said.

"Flowerfox," Moon called back in a wavy whisper. "Good evening. How are you faring these fine days?"

Flowerfox loved the sound of Moon talking. He couldn't describe it, but it made him want to sing fox songs that had never been heard before. He shivered slightly. Being with Moon at night always made him feel things that were hard to feel in the daytime. Just as he was about to speak, he caught the ghost of a sweet, low chuckle from Moon. He sighed. Why was he always so tongue-tied in moonlight?

"Ah," he said, just to make the moment last. "Ah, what you do to me, Moon."

"So, Fox, life is still good, then?" Moon replied.

"Life. Life is always good, especially when you're here, Moon."

Moon laughed again. "I am always here, somewhere, dear Flowerfox. You may not see me, but I am always here, somewhere."

Flowerfox puzzled over this. "Are you trying to make my head hurt?"

"Oh, little fox. I do love you. I love others, though, too, you know, and sometimes I must show my face to them. You know about taking turns, right?"

Flowerfox sighed again. "Yes, of course, I know. And maybe if I could see you like this every night, it wouldn't mean as much to me...though that is hard to imagine." He blinked hard; all that moonlight had made him forget his eyes were getting dry. "Moon, when I'm with you like this, I feel things. I see things in my head. I want to do things. I want to stay still and not move and not breathe. Why is that?"

"Because," Moon said, and the barest sensation of Moon's touch ran along the tips of the fox's fur, "you are alive, and you love being alive, and I remind you of parts of being alive that you forget in the day."

Something welled up in Flowerfox's throat and escaped in another sigh. He didn't know why he kept doing that.

"You're getting older, Flowerfox," Moon said, gently. "Your world is changing. You'll find out very soon just how much. You can't see what I can see."

"I *know* the world is changing. Now the leaves are green; soon they will be yellow, then red, then brown—"

"Not *the* world," Moon interrupted. "*Your* world."

"You *are* trying to make my head hurt, Moon. I love you, but you confuse me," and Flowerfox shook his head to dispel the uneasiness of not understanding.

"Hush," Moon said. "It's all right. You'll understand when it's time."

Waves of moonlove washed over and through Flowerfox, and suddenly he felt he didn't need to wonder or worry or figure anything out. He felt utterly still and completely, electrically energized. He felt every tiny part of him wake up and then be peaceful.

Moon climbed higher in the sky, trailing long sweeps of cloud, until Flowerfox couldn't see even the trails anymore. And although he usually hunted at night and then returned to one of the pack's dens, he stayed right there. As hours passed and the shadows crept over him, he fell asleep.

Moss and Flowerfox

Flowerfox had many friends among the foxes, as many as among the not-foxes. One was Moss. Neither a littermate nor an elder, Moss was in the same pack and had crossed his path often from the time they were old enough to leave their dens—which was about the same time for each.

Flowerfox was sometimes surprised to see her because he never heard her coming. Foxes were capable of silence and most often made little sound, but Moss was beyond capable. It was said her mother had not known she was coming until she was there, and none among the foxes doubted it. Moss was just that quiet. Her motions were not just stealthy; they were invisible. She was not there, and then there, and then gone. Just like that.

Flowerfox woke from his sleep on the rock to a warm day. In fact, it was very warm. As he opened his eyes, he realized that another fox body with the softest fur and a fragrance unlike any other was curled next to him. He blinked, and yawned, and stretched.

"Morning, Moss," Flowerfox said. Moss's golden eyes gazed back at him so directly it would have been unnerving if it hadn't been comforting; she had always known him better than the other foxes. She rooted through the fur on his side to the skin beneath.

"Morning, Flowerfox," she replied, pulling her sniffing snout out of his fur. "You need to hunt."

"How would you know?" said Flowerfox, sitting up and letting his fur ruffle in the breeze. "You don't know everything I do."

"No, but I can smell almost as well as you, and I can feel just as well," she retorted softly, "and I can smell your empty stomach, and feel your ribs a little too much. You need to eat; therefore, you need to hunt."

Flowerfox yawned again. She was right; he had not hunted the night before, being absorbed in talking with Moon, and his hunger hadn't made itself known...until now. He hated when she was right.

"Well," he said, "I was waiting till I was really hungry. Food tastes better then."

Moss nipped him playfully, which caught him off guard. "I know where there's a nest of eggs ready to crack...and where some fish are hiding. *Maybe* I could be convinced to show you."

Flowerfox caught her ear gently with his teeth, gave it a soft tug, and then let go. "I know where there's a cache of berries even the birds haven't found yet, and *maybe* I could be persuaded to share them with you."

She jumped off the rock first and almost melted into the woods, with her taste and smell hanging in the air just enough to pull Flowerfox after her before she disappeared.

They broke their fast with two eggs each and then found themselves at the stream's edge. The sunlight had not penetrated the shadows of the overhanging trees, and the foxes neatly caught several small fish each, disposing of them just as neatly. As always, Flowerfox was impressed by Moss's speed and efficiency, as well as her graceful alertness after eating. She sat, drawn into herself, tail tucked round her feet, seeming to take in the shadows, the sun and clouds, the way the water changed color endlessly, seeming without trying to melt into the day. He, on the other hand, could not resist rolling in the high grasses, giving a long noisy sniff, and then grunting and sighing in satisfaction.

"I was promised berries," Moss admonished him.

Flowerfox let out a huff and wiggled his back against the grasses. "Always hungry," he complained mildly. "And I didn't promise."

"Nor did I," said Moss as she raised one spread paw to inspect between her toes.

"Oh, all right," said Flowerfox, and rolled over. He stood and stretched. "Are vixens always thinking about food? Can't you just enjoy the moment for once?"

Moss lowered her paw. "I eat when I can," she sniffed, "because there are times when I can't. And berries sound perfect just now, speaking of enjoying the moment."

Flowerfox wanted a nap, but he felt a bit shamed; he knew Moss had been the smallest pup in her litter, and the hungriest. He decided he could just as well nap with a belly full of berries. In one leap he bounded off, knowing Moss would be beside him.

When they got there, he was relieved to see the cache was still bountiful. Had they waited, the birds would have got them; as it was, he let Moss take the bigger share. He wasn't that hungry anymore, anyway, and Moss had never outgrown her enormous appetite. He plopped down in the grass and watched her eat.

"Moss," he asked her, "do you ever talk to Moon?'

She gulped and tidily licked juice off her snout. "Well, of course," she said, looking at him quizzically. "I thought we all did."

Flowerfox didn't quite know what to say. He looked away; his talks with Moon were unlike any other conversations he had with anyone, and to hear that talking with Moon was so commonplace disturbed him. He thought a moment. "No, I mean...*talk*. I mean, say things and hear things you don't with anyone else."

This got her attention. "Ah, like that," she said. She lay down, put her head on her paws, and looked at him steadily. She didn't seem focused on berries anymore. "Well, yes, sometimes. It's probably different for me, but yes, sometimes."

"Hmmm." Flowerfox considered this and what he wanted to say next. Moss was his oldest not-littermate friend, and he wanted to be careful. He sighed. "It's just that... some of the things Moon says confuse me. Last night, Moon told me that my world was going to change very soon and that I couldn't see what Moon could see."

Moss took her time answering, and something in her eyes unsettled Flowerfox. "Yes, I know. Moon told me that, too, but I knew already."

Flowerfox was about to ask, "Knew what, exactly?" But from the corner of his eye, he saw the grass part off toward the trees and a rabbit leap to run from some hunter; at the same moment, a swift shadow passed from overhead, and a hawk plummeted down toward the fleeing animal, its wingtips almost touching Flowerfox's head as they beat down. He froze—he loved the taste of rabbit, but he was full and wasn't interested in stealing from a hawk—and in that moment, he forgot what he wanted to ask. When he shook himself out of his paralysis, Moss was still looking at him steadily.

"Thanks for the berries," she said quietly, and with a single small movement, turned and melted back into the woods. This time, he did not follow.

Flowerfox and Moon Howler

There was a place where humans lived that Flowerfox considered an unofficial part of his territory. Foxes found food there, but they also found humans; and stories had been handed down about what happened to foxes that were found by humans there. Flowerfox knew there were times it was safer to go there and, perhaps, scout for food humans had thrown out, or check the chicken coop for holes in the wire. Flowerfox had occasionally seen one, just big enough to reach in and scoop out an egg or three, which he would eat as fast as he could before slipping off. But the humans seemed to find these holes, too, and patch them up quickly.

There had also been a dog litter recently. Flowerfox had watched the pups grow, marveling at how similar they were to fox pups, sometimes wondering if they were actually some kind of fox humans had tamed. They looked different, but they acted so similar. This made him curious and think that he might meet one someday. He was right.

One evening just after moonrise, Flowerfox was on his way to a little rise where he could see Moon. The sky was not fully dark just yet, and the summer air was full of sounds and smells that made his nose twitch. He had eaten enough and didn't feel drawn to hunting just then. He neared the rise and stopped. Someone had got there first; he smelled dog—both like and unlike fox. Both curious and wary, Flowerfox stealthily crept nearer until he could see the shadow of the dog. He waited, considering his options.

"I know you're there," came a low growl. "I won't hurt you if you won't hurt me."

Flowerfox straightened up, tail high, and trotted over to the dog. "Sounds good to me," he replied. He took a seat a few feet away, so he could see and move quickly if the dog changed its mind.

The dog turned to him and sniffed. "I've seen you around my humans' farm," he said. "You should be careful."

Flowerfox sniffed too. "I am. My name is Flowerfox, by the way."

"Mine is Mutt," said the dog gruffly.

"Mutt?" Flowerfox was surprised. "What does that mean?"

"What it says," Mutt said, and looked away. "I imagine foxes 'round here are all... the same kind of fox, but dogs aren't all the same kind of dog. Mutt means lots of kinds of dog, all mixed together in one dog."

Flowerfox looked at Mutt. Mutt was only a little taller than he was; his fur was short and grizzled. In the moonlight, it was impossible to tell what colors he was. Mutt's ears were rounded and long enough that they flopped over. And Flowerfox saw that Mutt was male and wore a collar around his neck, the kind of thing humans used to mark the animals they decided belonged to them. Flowerfox felt a little sorry for him. He knew humans were frightening and dangerous; and he couldn't imagine living with them, which made him even more curious than usual.

"What is it like, living with humans?" he asked.

Mutt yawned and scratched his ear. "It's pretty good. They feed me and play with me, and scratch my belly and pet me. They let me in the house to sleep, but sometimes I just need to get out. I love my humans, but tonight I just needed to get out. I have a hole under the fence they haven't found yet. They'll find it and fill it in, but until then, I can roam a little." He raised his snout to the moon. "If I howl, they'll hear me and call me in. I really want to howl, but I also want to be out a little longer."

"Howling is more fun when Moon is up," said Flowerfox. "Moon likes us to howl. But until then, we can just sit here if you like. I know humans are dangerous, but why exactly did you tell me to be careful?"

"They're worried about their chickens," said Mutt. "They're mostly nice and *not* dangerous, but they have a gun, and they say they'll shoot any animal that comes after the chickens. They expect me to guard them, too. So if they saw you and they didn't see me chasing you away, they would get the gun and try to shoot you. Not that I would blame you for chasing the chickens, mind you. They're not as smart as we are, and they're fun to chase."

Flowerfox shivered; it was an old story, handed down among all the wild things. Humans had weapons and could maim and kill any animal they chose. "Thanks for the warning," he said. "I wouldn't want to put you in that position, and I certainly wouldn't want to get shot. But the ones you should look out for are Bawbbikat and the Coyote clan. They won't be so easily warned off."

Moon started to come up over the horizon. Flowerfox knew it was almost howling time. "I would like to be friends," he told Mutt. "Do you think we can?"

Mutt seemed to think for a moment. "It would be good to have a friend outside the fence. I would like that. Just don't make me choose between you and my humans."

Flowerfox agreed.

They watched Moon come up, all the way up, into the sky. Together, they gathered themselves and howled. It was magnificent.

"I'd better go," said Mutt. He stood and began to turn away.

"I think you need a new name," said Flowerfox. "I shall call you Moonhowler."

Moonhowler touched noses with Flowerfox and ran off, yipping. Flowerfox yipped back. Now other howls filled the night air—and the sound of human voices calling. Flowerfox looked at Moon and thought he saw a wink. It was barely there, and he didn't know how it could have happened, but it had.

Flowerfox and Rowandoe Eat Apples

The days had lengthened, and Flowerfox had soaked in as much sunlight as he could; game had been plentiful, and berries, too. He noticed leaves and grasses turning from green to yellow, and the hours of sunlight shortening. It was still warm—in fact, it still sometimes was so hot he retreated to curl up and nap in shade for hours during the day—but now, in addition to the late berries, his nose brought him news of the year's crop of early apples. He decided to visit his favorite spot of ancient apple trees, which legend told had been planted by humans and then, for whatever reason, abandoned, the way humans sometimes abandoned things. Suddenly hungry and salivating, he moved off to where he knew he would be rewarded.

Flowerfox found apples already fallen but not yet starting to rot. These were easy pickings, though he didn't mind jumping for the treat of a juicy, sweet tart apple. He had eaten five (they were small) when a new scent and a gentle shadow alerted him to a visitor. He turned, juice dripping from his muzzle, and swallowed.

"Afternoon, Rowandoe," he greeted her.

Rowandoe picked her way gracefully to his side. "Greetings, Flowerfox," she said. "I should remember I can never surprise you." She moved her head to pull an apple off a low-hanging branch with her teeth, and then she regarded him as she ate it. "Mmmm. There's nothing like these apples."

"I agree!" replied Flowerfox. They munched companionably for a few minutes. Small flies buzzed around them, and they flicked their tails in tandem, swatting them away.

Flowerfox realized his belly was full and lay down to digest. He gazed at Rowandoe and sniffed, curiously.

"Your spots," he said. "They've faded."

"Yes," she said. She harvested another apple.

"And," he said slowly, "you smell...different."

She chewed and swallowed. "Do I? Hmmm. I suppose I must."

"And I know we've both grown up a lot, but you seem very different...at least to me."

She laughed. The sound was surprising. "You're very perceptive. You know, you're very different, too."

He cocked his head. "Why is that?"

"Really, Flowerfox? You really don't know?"

This mystified him. He opened his mouth and closed it again.

"I am to find a mate soon," Rowandoe informed him, "as are you."

"Mate?" His voice was soft. He had only been a pup a season or two ago, although that seemed a long time to his fox mind.

She looked at him and shook her head. She pulled another apple down. Rowandoe could eat a lot of apples.

"When?" was all he could think of to say.

"Soon. Very soon, for me. The bucks are already getting restless. Soon they will be fighting all the time. It's a bit silly, but they take it very seriously, and sometimes they actually hurt each other."

Flowerfox had seen bucks fighting, usually half in play, but not always. It was something he had wisely decided to stay away from. When bucks were fighting, they seemed to lose sight of everything and everyone else around them—except to attack anyone in their way. That made it risky to go near them.

"Don't worry," Rowandoe reassured him. "It has nothing to do with you, really...except the mating part. It will be your turn to find a vixen soon. I've a feeling she'll find you, though."

"Oh, I hope so," Flowerfox said fervently. "I don't want to fight."

"No one *wants* to fight," she said. "Sometimes we *have* to fight, though I usually run. After I have fawns, that could change."

Flowerfox felt distinctly unsettled, but Rowandoe seemed so calm; this unsettled him even more somehow.

"Anyway," she said, "I'm not worried about it. I still have a few weeks before it all starts, I think." She ate one last apple. "Oh, those are so good. I want more, but I'm full." She folded her long legs beneath her and settled into the grass. One ear flicked as a fly buzzed by it. She let out a gentle snort and closed her eyes.

Flowerfox lay a long time, thinking. A small green snake slithered by, but he didn't want to eat. He was still too full and too unsettled. Moon had been right—his world was changing. He didn't know what to think of that, of Rowandoe bearing fawns, of him fathering pups; he had only taken care of himself, so far, though he had shared some of his kills with the pack. Eventually, he stood, stretched, and shook himself all over. He flicked his tail and prepared to trot off; when his brain got too full, he knew it was time to move.

Just as he took his first step, Rowandoe opened her eyes.

"It will be fine," she told him. "We're made for this. Who knows, we might even like it."

Flowerfox didn't know quite what to say, so he nodded and left.

Moss Meets Moonhowler

It was a full moon in autumn; the night was dry and clear. Flowerfox found his favorite rock and settled in. He expected that Moss would join him—she knew all his favorite places; and on these longer, colder nights, they were accustomed to curling up together. Generally she found him, rather than the other way around; he had the distinct feeling she liked her time to herself.

Flowerfox and Moon greeted one another. "Ah," Moon said, "I see you're alone."

"For now," he replied.

"Yes," Moon said. "You aren't alone as often anymore."

Flowerfox shrugged. "I suppose not. I guess I'm used to being with Moss now. It just...happened."

"As these things do," said Moon. "You two will be denning soon."

Flowerfox shivered. "I haven't thought about that," he said offhandedly. He didn't want Moon to know he wasn't sure he was ready for that yet.

"Why does the idea of denning with Moss make you uncomfortable?"

He shook himself. "It...doesn't," he protested feebly. Moon didn't respond. He blew out a sigh. "It does," he finally said. "I know what denning means." He took a breath.

"It's just that I just *was* a pup. I don't know about having them, taking care of them."

37

"It's not as if you'll be doing it alone," Moon chided him, gently. "And is Moss not a good companion to you?"

"Oh yes, oh yes," Flowerfox told Moon.

"And do you enjoy being with her?"

"Yes, of course. Moon—you said my world was changing. Is this what you meant?"

"Has it been changing?"

Moon was teasing him, he knew. "Yes!"

"Well, then, that's part of what I meant."

Flowerfox felt tender around his heart, and not in the mood for Moon's riddles. "What else, then?"

A shiver of Moon's light ran through him. "I cannot tell you everything at once," Moon said softly. "You have to let it come to you. It will, in time. All of it."

He couldn't speak. What did she mean? He was feeling very uneasy. He wished Moss was there.

"I will tell you this," Moon continued. "What is between you and Moss will always be one of the best things in your life."

Just then, Flowerfox sensed the air shift on either side of him, and not one but two familiar scents. Moss materialized on one side, very close, and Moonhowler on the other, further away. Both were bristling. Moss spoke first.

"He's *chasing* me," said Moss. "I would have brought you a treat, but he wouldn't leave me alone." A low growl escaped her throat.

"Flowerfox," said Moonhowler, just as gruffly, "is this vixen with you? Have you told her about our agreement?"

"Not yet," Flowerfox said, reluctantly. He had meant to, but there was always something else going on.

"Not yet!" Moonhowler was just barely holding his temper. "Vixen—"

"Moss," interrupted Flowerfox quickly. He could feel Moss's tension rising even higher. "—your friend Flowerfox here," Moonhowler told Moss, "agreed to leave the chickens alone and never make me choose between him and my humans. If you want me to leave you alone, you'll have to promise the same." He looked ready to lunge; Flowerfox glanced at him, and Moonhowler stayed in check. "I only chased her because I thought it might be you, and I wanted to find out why you didn't stay away," he grunted.

"Moss," said Flowerfox, turning to her, "please listen. Moonhowler is a friend to me, and he can be to you. The humans are dangerous, like all humans. They have a gun, and they'll use it on us if we don't stay away." In that moment, Flowerfox felt a cold fear; the thought of humans killing Moss was more than he could bear. "Please, promise. Please." He felt her freeze, and then, ever so slightly, relax. There was silence for a long, uncomfortable moment.

"I promise," she said to Moonhowler. "I *promise*," she told Flowerfox, and touched his nose with hers. He could see Moonhowler relax and move just a little closer, but not in a threatening way.

"I'm hungry, though," she told Flowerfox plaintively.

"You're always hungry," he said. "But I was talking with Moon. Do you want to stay, or hunt?"

"'Hello, Moon," Moss said. "I'll hunt and come back. I'll hunt *away* from the humans," she said with a glance at Moonhowler. And she was gone, melting into the shadows.

They watched her go. "Are you sure...?" Moonhowler began.

"I'm sure," Flowerfox assured him. "Once she makes a promise, she keeps it. She may not like it, but she'll stay away."

"Good, then. I have to get back," said Moonhowler. Flowerfox could tell he was still suspicious of Moss. "I might as well have a howl while I'm out here."

He and Flowerfox raised their voices to the sky, and Flowerfox felt better; he hoped his friend did too.

And later, after Moonhowler raced home, Moss brought Flowerfox a tender rabbit. They shared their meal and fell asleep in a hidden place while Moon silently crept across the sky.

Mating Season

Days were growing shorter and nights chilly. Flowerfox could see by the softening light of Sun and the changing colors of the leaves that summer was over. The berries were mostly gone now, and he didn't care for the way their thorns got caught in his fur and his nose when he went after the deepest hidden ones.

Flowerfox knew by the smells, and by something inside him, that his world was changing, and so was he. The very taste of the air had changed, and he didn't know how much of that was him, and how much the world around him. He enjoyed the new smells and colors, but he had a sense that things would never be as easy, and as free, for him as they had once been.

The bigger wild ones, the Coyote clan, were circling closer these days, and among the foxes there had been an alert swiftly passed that cougar and wolves were not far away and getting closer too. Also, Flowerfox was hearing more guns, and those noises were not comforting.

Flowerfox started to feel hungrier, day by day. He hunted more, and more often than not, Moss hunted with him. Between hunts, they rolled in the meadows and played together, or just slept, curled up. It made for a change, but it felt right.

Other things changed, too. The antlered bucks kept tangling up in fights, and their noises broke the quiet. Flowerfox was fervently glad he had known to stay clear of them. Squirrels seemed more active—and fatter, making good meals when Flowerfox or Moss caught one. All the creatures around them seemed to be preparing for something, and the foxes knew that something was winter.

One day, Flowerfox and Moss met Rowandoe as they were scouting through the woods.

"Hello, Moss. Hello, Flowerfox," she greeted them.

"Rowandoe, you look different," Flowerfox said, tilting his head in curiosity. "I don't know why, but you do."

Moss huffed quietly, laughing.

"Of course she looks different," Moss chided him. "It's mating season."

Rowandoe tossed her head. "Yes."

Flowerfox felt a little stunned. "Does that mean you found a mate?"

Rowandoe looked at him steadily. "Yes. I'll have my own fawns in early spring."

Moss opened her mouth in a toothy grin. "That's wonderful, Rowandoe."

Flowerfox wasn't sure what to think. Maybe it *was* wonderful, but it was a big, big change. If Rowandoe was going to be a mother, she was grown up. And if she was grown up, then maybe he and Moss would be soon, too. He felt Moss's gaze and turned to her. Her eyes had an expression he hadn't noticed before, one that made him feel uncomfortable, kind of hot and prickly. He shook himself all over and let out a sigh.

"Well. Better be extra careful, then, Rowandoe. We heard a cougar scream yesterday, and there's talk of a pair of wolves heading this way. Take care of yourself."

Rowandoe dipped her head gracefully. "And you as well, Flowerfox. Moss, be safe. I'll see you soon." She walked off, blending into the forest as she went.

Flowerfox felt Moss's stare again and turned to her. "What?" he demanded. The hot, prickly feeling was back.

Moss huffed again. "Nothing. Maybe we should try the river—there might be some trout. Haven't had trout in a while." And she was off, in her silent Moss way.

The Local Lion

The nights grew colder and longer, and the skies stormy. Often there was rain, and sometimes frost. Sun seemed very far away much of the time. All the foxes had grown heavy coats. It was early winter, and Flowerfox was glad not to be going through it alone.

One day when the woods were deep in shadow, he and Moss were pacing through the woods. They had just eaten, though not much; they had happened upon someone else's kill. The woods were quieter now, with less birdsong, and the ground was cold and damp. Moss paused—she had seen a flash through the trees and thought it was perhaps a rabbit, perhaps other prey—and Flowerfox froze, letting her take the lead. Suddenly they heard the scream of a cougar, far too close. Neither one moved. Moss melted back behind a tree, staying close to the ground; Flowerfox did his best to emulate her. Neither one wanted to tangle with a cougar.

The cougar screamed again, and a young buck burst through the clearing; the cougar leaped after him, and both were gone.

Flowerfox thought of Rowandoe and hoped she was safe, away from there. He and Moss turned in the opposite direction and began to lope away. They headed for a meadow where they could hope to flush out a rabbit or some other small creature. They had almost made it out of the woods when they heard a familiar voice.

"Hello, my fox friends," Bawbbikat greeted them. Her voice floated down from a tree branch where she curled, watchful but somehow still relaxed. "I take it you heard our local lion."

They looked up at her. "Do you know that cougar?" Flowerfox asked.

"I do," she said. "Not to speak to, mind you, but I know him, and he me. And I stay out of his way, as I advise both of you to do the same."

"Well, that's what we're doing," Moss informed her. "How are you faring, Bawbbikat?" Moss tended not to use titles; she preferred being more direct. This made Flowerfox nervous sometimes, but even Bawbbikat didn't seem to mind.

"Hunting is good," Bawbbikat said, and yawned. Her teeth were always impressive. "There's enough for all of us. It should be a good winter. Not too much frost yet, but there will be soon, and snow." She seemed pleased, even purring a little.

Just then, a movement parted the dried grasses of the meadow, and Moss leaped after it before Flowerfox could react. Bawbbikat told him, "Go! There are more. Don't make your vixen do *all* the hunting."

He ran. Moss had indeed flushed a rabbit, and another sprang off in the opposite direction. It led Flowerfox a fast chase through the meadow before he caught and killed it. Although he was salivating, Flowerfox took his kill back to Moss, who had already started her meal.

When they had finished, they rolled in the grasses. "Bawbbikat's right," said Moss. "Snow is coming." Then she curled against Flowerfox and fell asleep.

Flowerfox tucked his nose under his tail and fell asleep too, but not before wondering. He knew foxes were starting to den. He spared a thought for the prospect, but he was too full to linger on it for long. He too fell asleep.

Denning, Part 1

Flowerfox awoke and couldn't find Moss anywhere. Although this wasn't that unusual, suddenly it felt that way, and he wondered why. He felt different somehow.

He sat up, yawned, and shook himself all over. It was cold and he could see frost, but the sky was clear. He sniffed, trying to get his bearings. What was different? And where was Moss?

Flowerfox set off, tracking. He didn't even realize he was doing it at first. Moss usually found him, but this time he felt the need to find her. He tracked through the meadow and into the woods. He tracked to the edge of the river, and to where the last few shriveled berries clung to their thorny vines; suddenly he heard a sound, an odd cry, and smelled something both familiar and strange. It was Moss, and not Moss, under a tree, pacing.

"Moss—" he started to greet her, and stopped. They looked at each other. Flowerfox felt something turn inside him. Her scent was musky, and he had to get closer. She didn't run. Her eyes were different.

Suddenly Flowerfox was by her, on her, with that scent in his nose and mouth. It was over very fast.

She nipped him and started cleaning her fur. He shook his head, wondering. She was Moss again, and he was Flowerfox. They had been someone, something else, together, for a moment. It had

47

happened so fast and now, he knew what would happen, yet somehow, he wasn't scared. At least, he wasn't *too* scared.

"We need our own den," he told her. They sat down together, very close.

"I know," she said. She nipped him again. "I've already found one."

Flowerfox knew better than to be surprised, but he was anyway. "Where?"

"I'll show you," she said. "It's a big one, and we won't have to dig too much. My sisters have their dens in the same place." She got up to go.

"Wait," Flowerfox protested. "Right now?"

"Right now," Moss told him. "It's very safe. You'll like it." She turned and he followed.

Moss was right; he did like it. He was pleased that they didn't have to dig the entire den themselves. It was already dug into the side of small hill, mostly hidden by tree roots, fallen branches, and rocks. Inside, it was dark and warm, with enough room for them to create their own hollow. He could smell the other foxes and knew he would get to know them soon. He realized that once Moss had her pups, there would be a lot of bodies in there, and somehow that was comforting. It surprised him to be comforted at that; he had so enjoyed being on his own and then just being with Moss. He must have changed, but he didn't know when.

They dug their hollow a little deeper, and then they rested, curled up together. Everything felt different. When they awoke a few hours later and ventured outside, everything looked different, too. It was evening, and the sky had clouded over. He could smell a deeper frost coming, and maybe more, maybe even snow.

Everything was different now.

Denning, Part II

They settled in to live with Moss's sisters and their mates—one of whom was a littermate of his, called Minkbane. It felt right to Flowerfox, being with this part of his pack rather than another.

As for Moss, she explained, "This is the den I was born in. My sisters and I hunted to help our mother feed us all, especially our brothers." He knew that was true, and that her brothers had gone, just as he had, to find their own mates and dens. He was grateful to share her home.

Moss got thicker. Her belly grew heavy and eventually, it slowed her down, something Flowerfox had somehow never believed would happen. She was still a better, and quieter, hunter than he–just not faster. He took this as a sign, a warning, maybe. Their pups were coming soon, so he worked harder at finding food and bringing it back to her. He tried to learn her hunting ways, and thought of hunting more as practice than he ever had, wanting to be as good at it as he could. As for Moss, she spent time piling up masses of dead leaves and began to fashion a nest with them.

One day in late winter, Moss wouldn't leave the den. She paced, then curled up in the leaf nest, then stretched out. Her breathing changed. Flowerfox, alarmed, asked what was wrong.

"Nothing," she huffed, but her eyes were narrowed and she was breathing hard. He saw Minkbane slipping by on the way out of the den and followed him.

"Minkbane, this isn't like Moss. She can't seem to settle down, and she won't leave the den, and she's breathing hard. What should I do?"

Minkbane turned to him. "You really don't know?"

"No, what am I supposed to know? Tell me!" Flowerfox was starting to feel panicky.

"She's bearing the pups."

Flowerfox suddenly felt terrified, and then very, very calm. He stopped breathing, gulped in some air, shook himself, and said, "What do I do?"

Minkbane seemed to warm for a moment. "Hunt. She'll need food." And he turned to go, because his mate, too, needed food to nurse their pups.

Flowerfox turned back into the den. He found Moss, breathing heavily, eyes mostly closed. He licked her ears and said, "I'm going hunting. I'll bring you food."

Moss grunted and closed her eyes completely.

It took some time, but Flowerfox found a relatively lethargic squirrel and brought it back, dangling from his jaws. He laid it on the ground of the den near Moss.

"Not here," she rasped. "Move it over there instead."

He wasn't even bothered that she didn't thank him. He watched her for a while, and then he went out to feed himself.

He hunted and ate in the snow, and tracked back to the den, letting his nose lead him, since everything was now covered in white. Moss had changed position and was furiously licking a tiny dark bundle, slick, wet, and wiggly. When Flowerfox's eyes had adjusted, he realized it was a pup; he couldn't tell whether it was a female or a male. Awed, he sniffed the baby, moved back, and hunkered down to wait.

It seemed to take a long time, but maybe it didn't. When it was all done, Moss had given birth to five pups, three females and two males. As she lay nursing them, Flowerfox pushed the dead squirrel closer to her head. She looked at him; he knew she was exhausted, but there was a light in her eyes. He nuzzled her head. They were silent for a while, listening to the pups suckle and mewl.

"I'm glad that's over," Moss said, quietly. "Thanks for the food." She didn't even have the energy to nip him.

"Me too," agreed Flowerfox. "They're beautiful, Moss." She didn't answer, and he realized she had fallen asleep while nursing the pups. He watched as the babies seemed to tuck themselves into her and each other, and one by one, fell asleep too.

Flowerfox could feel the vibration of the wind outside. He turned his back to the den entrance, curled himself around the pups to touch Moss, and closed his eyes. In a few moments he, too, was asleep.

Days went by, then weeks. Flowerfox hunted and brought his kill back to the den; and he hunted and brought it back again, over and over. Moss seemed so hungry all the time, and he was, too. The pups grew so fast it was a blur. Later in spring, Moss stood, stretched, and began to shove them out of the den. They tumbled over each other, protesting in little yips and yaps. Moss picked up the last one by its scruff and carried it out. She dropped it on the ground casually and started off in the direction of water. She was thirsty.

"Time for your first look at the world," she told the pups.

They were only out for a short while, but it was enough that Flowerfox could see the pups were curious and energetic. This was good, as not only would they have to learn to like being out in the world, he wanted them to love it as he did.

Flowerfox began shepherding the pups from time to time so Moss could hunt; she liked getting out, and she wanted to hunt, so they took turns. The weather was turning toward summer, though still chilly in the mornings. Moss began taking some of the pups—mostly the vixens—with her to hunt. He took the males with him to hunt, too; but somehow Moss and the little vixens always brought home more. There was enough to eat, and the pups grew so fast that Flowerfox began to wonder if he had ever been so big and strong at their age—whatever age they were on whatever day he wondered. As the days lengthened and warmed, he realized they would be hunting for themselves soon, and he and Moss would have to teach them.

Maybe Moss realized that, too, because she went out more and more on her own, as if to get used to the idea that the pups would soon not need her anymore. She began to seem more like the old Moss, vanishing and then reappearing at times, but always coming back to the den. They had already brought their pups to meet the rest of the pack, and some of Flowerfox's friends. Flowerfox and Moss played with their pups in the meadows and the woods. The pups seemed to have endless energy, until they just stopped in their tracks and fell asleep, needing their parents to carry them back to the den. Eventually they learned to go back to the den, or find a hiding place, to sleep in. Flowerfox had made an agreement with Bawbbikat that kept her from attacking the pups, but there were still other hunters he didn't trust; he knew that any cougar was a threat, not to mention coyotes and wolves.

Even hawks and eagles were dangerous to fox pups, and both Flowerfox and Moss had lost siblings to them. But soon this was a bit less of a worry. Their pups had grown fast and were healthy and strong—except for one male, who had always been a bit smaller and slower than the others. They called this pup Sweeteyes for his sweet disposition. He was the one they worried about the most, and in a way, their dearest fox child.

Denning, Part III

It was now high summer. The whole family was out hunting, but first they stopped to talk to Sun. Flowerfox never tired of showing off the pups.

"It's good to see you so happy in being a father," Sun told him approvingly, as the fox children wandered off, following their noses, being watched and followed by Moss. Flowerfox noticed how Moss, as always, kept an especially close watch on Sweeteyes, and he knew he'd have to cut the conversation short.

"I am," said Flowerfox, "and it's good to know you approve." He couldn't relax, though, and bade his old friend goodbye.

"Take care," Sun cautioned him. "Everyone is out today. Everyone."

Flowerfox later wished he had taken Sun's words more to heart.

As they roamed and the fox children practiced stalking, somehow Sweeteyes, not for the first time, got separated from the others. Flowerfox and Moss discovered this just as the rest had stopped at the edge of a clearing in the woods.

"I'll go," she told Flowerfox. She turned and melted back the way they had come. Flowerfox gathered the other pups and told them to wait. He took a long look back where Moss had vanished. Something didn't feel quite right.

Suddenly, the fur on the back of his neck seemed to stand up, and he froze, listening. Something was very wrong. Then he heard the chilling scream of a cougar, Moss growling a warning, Sweeteyes yipping frantically—and the yipping stop in mid-voice. Flowerfox shoved the other pups into a tree snag, told them to stay, and ran.

It was all over by the time he got there. He could see where the cougar had taken Sweeteyes; both were gone, and blood was on the ground. He could see Moss lying still, so still. She had fought hard, but she had lost. She was gashed horribly and bleeding, as Sweeteyes had bled; somehow he knew she was dying. She could not move; she could only look at Flowerfox, her eyes losing light as she gazed at him, her breath coming ragged.

"Moss," he cried, and dropped down next to her. He tried to wrap himself around her. "Moss," he cried again, more quietly this time.

"I tried," she rasped. "I tried, Flowerfox..."

"Moss," he whispered. He had never felt such anguish. He licked her face.

"Take the pups home, Flowerfox," she said, and then said no more. Her breathing slowed, and then stopped.

Flowerfox nudged her, but she was gone. He lifted his head and howled, then howled again.

After

Flowerfox howled until he coughed, mad with grief. At some awful moment, he realized the pups had left the tree snag and were surrounding him and Moss's body, whining, sniffing, confused. He looked around at them and realized he had to get them home because the cougar would be back. Yet he hated to leave Moss, knowing he would never see her again, knowing that would make it real for the rest of his life. Nothing else seemed to matter.

It wasn't just the pups who had arrived, however. Minkbane, Moss's sister Russet, and other pack members had arrived; and so Flowerfox had help, though he could barely look at anyone but Moss.

"Flowerfox," Minkbane said; he was standing close, saying his name over and over, and had been for a while. "Flowerfox, I know. Who did this?"

"The cougar," Flowerfox managed to choke out. "I want to take her home."

"You can't," Minkbane told him. "The cougar will come back for her body. We have to get out of here, all of us."

"Then I'll stay."

"No," said Russet. "Moss would want you to go home with the pups."

She spoke firmly, but with a quaver, and Flowerfox realized she was grieving too. Suddenly he remembered: Moss had said to take them home; Russet was right. "Then I'm taking her, too."

He closed his eyes. The pack came to a decision. "We'll help you," said Minkbane. "But we have to hurry."

Moss was heavy in death, so Minkbane helped Flowerfox carry her body. Russet and two other vixens corralled the surviving pups and led them back to the den; other pack members guarded Flowerfox and Minkbane. Somehow they all made it; the pack members walking behind did their best to scuff away the blood trail as they went.

Inside the den, Flowerfox couldn't think. It had taken everything in him to get that far, and now he didn't know what to do next. He kept licking Moss, somehow comforted by the action. The pups sniffed her, whined, and cried. Russet and Minkbane sat with them, and eventually took the pups away to distract them.

At some point later, Flowerfox could think again, but all he could think was, *Why?* Why hadn't he gone after Sweeteyes? Then he would be dead, and Moss alive, and he wouldn't be feeling as if a predator had scooped out his insides; it would have already happened, and he would feel nothing, ever again. Why had they been in that part of the woods right then? Why was the cougar even there right then?

Flowerfox stayed in the den, with Moss, the rest of the day and the whole night after. He barely noticed Minkbane slip out to hunt, and then slip back in. Minkbane laid a dead rabbit on the den floor near Flowerfox; Flowerfox didn't move.

In the morning, a large shadow fell across the den opening, and then moved toward Flowerfox. He tensed and looked up. It was an old fox—Flowerfox's father, Rogue, who had taught Flowerfox to hunt, who had a scar across his face from a close call with a younger, weaker cougar and a nicked ear from a human's bullet, who had visited his grandpups from time to time.

He moved over next to Flowerfox and sat down.

"Flowerfox," he said. They touched noses. "Flowerfox, I am so sorry. I know how you feel."

"Do you?" said Flowerfox. "Because I don't. I feel numb, and scared, and sad, and so angry. And I keep thinking it was my fault."

Rogue nodded. "Yes. I know."

"Stop saying that! How could you know?"

Rogue let out a sigh. "Because I've lost mates...and pups. It is the way things are. But you are still alive."

"I don't want to be!" Flowerfox barked. "I don't want to be alive if this is what being alive is! It hurts too much!"

"Yes," Rogue said. "It does. And somehow, we stay alive when it does... most of us, anyway."

"How?" It was almost a howl.

"One moment at a time," Rogue said, "even though it hurts...even though it hurts too much."

"But why?" Nothing made sense to Flowerfox anymore.

There was a pause; Rogue seemed to be thinking. Then he said, "Because you have other pups. Because they need you and the pack needs you. Because Sun keeps shining, and Moon keeps rising, and the seasons don't stop coming. Because we are, just as they are."

Thinking of the other pups, Flowerfox felt even guiltier. He had to take care of the other pups. He had to do it, not because he wanted to right now, but because Moss would have wanted him to. And Sweeteyes—Sweeteyes would have wanted it, too.

"Flowerfox," his father said gruffly, "it wasn't your fault. You and Moss did well, very well. Many pups don't survive. You kept them warm, and fed, and loved. You gave them all you could. And if you *had* gone after Sweeteyes, what would have happened if Moss had gone after the cougar? She had a temper, after all; she was always brave, but not always wise. And then the other pups could have all died, right there in the woods, when the cougar came back."

Flowerfox seemed to wake up. Rogue was right, even though it didn't make him feel any better.

"But what do I do now?" he asked his father, humbly.

"You say goodbye, Son," said Rogue, with gentleness. "You say goodbye."

It took a while even after that, but Flowerfox began to think. His father urged him to eat, and he ate some of the rabbit. After that he felt a little queasy, but he could move, and he was thinking better. He looked at Moss and realized she wasn't there anymore. He saw her body, but not her. He would never see her again.

Flowerfox, Rogue, and the other foxes conferred. Flowerfox wanted to bury the body, and they had to think of a place. Russet picked a spot where they could put the body into a crack in the big rocks near the river. It felt right to Flowerfox, and he consented.

In the late afternoon, they took the body to the rocks and laid it down next to the crack in the biggest boulder. Flowerfox licked the body all over, just once more; it still smelled like Moss, but more like death. "Moss," he said. "I love you. I miss you. Goodbye, Moss. And goodbye, Sweet-eyes. We all love you, and—I'm sorry." It was all he could say.

Russet had found wildflowers growing nearby. She pulled some up and scattered them on the body. And then Flowerfox, Minkbane, Russet, and Rogue pushed the body over the crack until it fell inside, and kicked what dirt, leaves, and debris they could over it. The pups helped with that part. They were all very quiet; no one whined or cried.

The burial over, the foxes stood back in a circle. Flowerfox held himself as erect as he could, and the pups barely moved. There was silence, and then Rogue raised the howl. They howled steadily for several minutes, and they heard howling back—dogs, coyotes, other fox packs. Flowerfox wondered whether Moonhowler was howling with them; he thought he must. Even the pups tried to howl, for the first time in their lives.

Finally they stopped. Rogue led them back to the den, the pups' home—the place where Moss was born. He made sure Flowerfox finished the rabbit. He stayed with Flowerfox another night and day, long enough to see Flowerfox curl up with his pups, and then he left. He knew Flowerfox would sleep now and would be all right, as hard as it was. He and the rest of the pack would see to that.

The End of Summer

It was a beautiful day, some weeks after Moss and Sweeteyes died. Flowerfox was hunting again, though he still felt sad and empty; hunting was necessary, but he did it as if in a dream. His surviving pups had recovered from the shock and were in and out of the den, often on their own now. He did his best for them, knowing that they were learning to survive on their own—as much as anyone ever did. Russet and Minkbane helped when needed; Rogue came around often, sometimes just sitting with Flowerfox, sometimes taking the pups hunting, sometimes bringing a kill over himself.

Flowerfox was still less motivated by hunger than by providing for his pups and denmates, so he had grown thinner. He still went to the woods and river; he kept Moss's grave covered as much as he could, but he could see the body deteriorating and knew not much would be left by winter. He stayed away from the clearing's edge where Moss had died and Sweeteyes had been taken. It was too hard to think about, most of the time, but he dreamed of it, and the dreams were not good. They woke him and made it hard for him to fall asleep again.

He sat near his favorite apple tree, not moving, barely thinking. Maybe he would take a nap. He could hear insects buzzing and birdsong, and then a rustle of something parting the grasses. And then he smelled deer.

Rowandoe, trailing two fawns, walked up to him.

"Flowerfox, I heard about Moss and Sweet-eyes," she told him. She looked him in the eyes. "I am so sorry."

"Thank you," he said, and looked away. "Your fawns look healthy, Rowandoe."

"Yes, they do, don't they? As do your pups. I see them all over now."

He laid his head on his paws, hunkering down, and his prominent bones jutted out of his skin. "They seem to be doing well."

Rowandoe looked at him, and her eyes went soft. "Flowerfox," she said, in a different voice. "Flowerfox, I'm glad you have no appetite for my fawns, but you must eat. When was your last meal?"

When had it been? There was a time when he ate constantly. That had been another life. Everything was different now, and he had grown accustomed to the ache in his belly, mostly eating what was left after everyone else ate, occasionally not eating at all.

Rowandoe pulled an apple down and rolled it in front of his nose. "Smell it, Flowerfox." He did, and surprisingly, he salivated. He couldn't remember the last time he smelled anything so good. He bit into it and ate it quickly, the juice running off his chin. He blinked and got up.

"I forgot how good these taste," he told her, and put his front paws on the tree to shake down more. There were so many, Rowandoe and her fawns helped him eat. Flowerfox realized he was still hungry. He needed more than apples; he needed meat.

"Thank you, Rowandoe," he told her. "I have to hunt now." She nodded.

He moved off into a meadow. He scouted carefully, putting his ear down to the ground in different places. He could hear movement and tracked it to a hole in the ground. He waited patiently, though he was now very hungry. Judging his moment, he leapt up and then down, lightning fast, and closed his jaws around a vole. Pulling it out, he ate it quickly. It wasn't enough, but it was a good snack. Maybe there were more?

Just for a few moments, hunting for himself took Flowerfox back to when he was a pup and worried about very little. It felt strange, but comforting. He missed that. He kept hunting; it took his mind off everything that hurt.

Flowerfox was late back to his den that night. He curled up with the pups and slept. He did not dream.

Sun Again, and Moon Again

The next day, Flowerfox went out. He tracked with Minkbane and the pups for a while, leading them through the woods and the meadow. They played and hunted through the afternoon. There had been no word of the cougar for a while, and they enjoyed their time. Eventually, they separated, some to keep roaming, some to return to the den, and Flowerfox was alone.

Flowerfox found himself sitting on a small rise; he could see mountains and meadows and woods, and the river, shining and shadowed, below. It was a beautiful day, he realized, a golden day on the cusp of autumn. He felt he had been asleep for weeks and completely missed the beauty that used to enthrall him. It felt so long since he had enjoyed himself, and today he had. He still felt sad, but now, he also felt grateful. And just a little tired. He wasn't a pup anymore, and keeping up with his brood made him realize how little energy he now had. That had to change.

It was warm and Sun hung lower in the sky, moving toward sunset and night.

"Hello, old friend," he greeted Sun.

"Greetings, Papa Flowerfox," Sun replied. "Are you well? I've been a bit worried about you."

"I am getting better, thank you, Sun," Flowerfox said, and huffed a small laugh. "Though I am not sure my pups need me much anymore," he admitted. And although he knew Sun had seen everything, he found himself telling the story of Moss and Sweeteyes. It felt good—better than he expected—to say their names, to tell the story of how they died.

"Yes," said Sun, thoughtfully. "I am sorry, Flowerfox. It is the way of things, but still, I am sorry, dear friend. I wish you all could have been spared."

"Thank you, Sun. I know you will be showing your face less from now on," Flowerfox replied, "so I'm grateful for our chat. I will try to see you more often."

"I look forward to that. I am very glad to see you," said Sun, "and grateful you are among the living."

They said goodbye, and Flowerfox stayed where he was. He watched Sun move beyond the horizon and the sky burst into flames and then darken. He then watched Moon rise.

"Dear, sweet Flowerfox," Moon greeted him. "I am so sorry about Moss and Sweeteyes."

"Thank you, Moon," Flowerfox said quietly. His throat seemed to close, and for a moment he couldn't speak.

"I know your heart is broken, dear fox, but are you and your other pups well?"

He sighed; this seemed to dislodge the blockage in his throat. "Yes. We are well. I am even eating again." This struck him as something he would not have said when Moss and Sweeteyes were alive. "And the night is still beautiful. And the world, and you."

He felt her beaming on him, through him, and shivered.

"So, it is still good to be alive, then?" Moon said, so gently.

"It is still good to be alive," he agreed. "And, Moon? You were right. I miss Moss, so much, and I am so glad she was with me, even for a little while. It was one of the best things in my life."

Just then he felt a presence by his side.

"Flowerfox," said Moonhowler gruffly, "I've been looking for you." He lowered his haunches next to Flowerfox. "I heard the howl. I heard about Moss and Sweeteyes. I'm sorry, Flowerfox."

Flowerfox looked at his friend and saw he meant it; he hadn't trusted Moss, but he was sorry. "Thank you," he said.

"I joined the howl," Moonhowler said. "My humans didn't like it. But then later, I couldn't find you."

"Here I am."

And they raised their voices to Moon, who listened and then watched as they ran, Flowerfox and Moonhowler, all the way to Moonhowler's fence. They said goodbye, and then Flowerfox went home, glancing once to tell Moon, "Thank you."

Moon heard, and paused a tiny moment to embrace it.

About the Author

Maria Orr is a Licensed Marriage and Family Therapist, writer, and artist who always knew she had a book in her. She gathers inspiration from nature, her art practice, and the strength and kindness of those around her, including her clients. She lives in Corvallis, Oregon, with her husband and their benevolent feline tyrant, Aengus Mac Og, who has been nagging her to write a book about *him*. You can see more of her art at https://www.silver-moonartsandpub.com/

CPSIA information can be obtained
at www.ICGtesting.com
Printed in the USA
BVHW021207060223
657964BV00005B/731